FORGOTTEN FACTS ABOUT LIFE ON A WAGON TRAIN

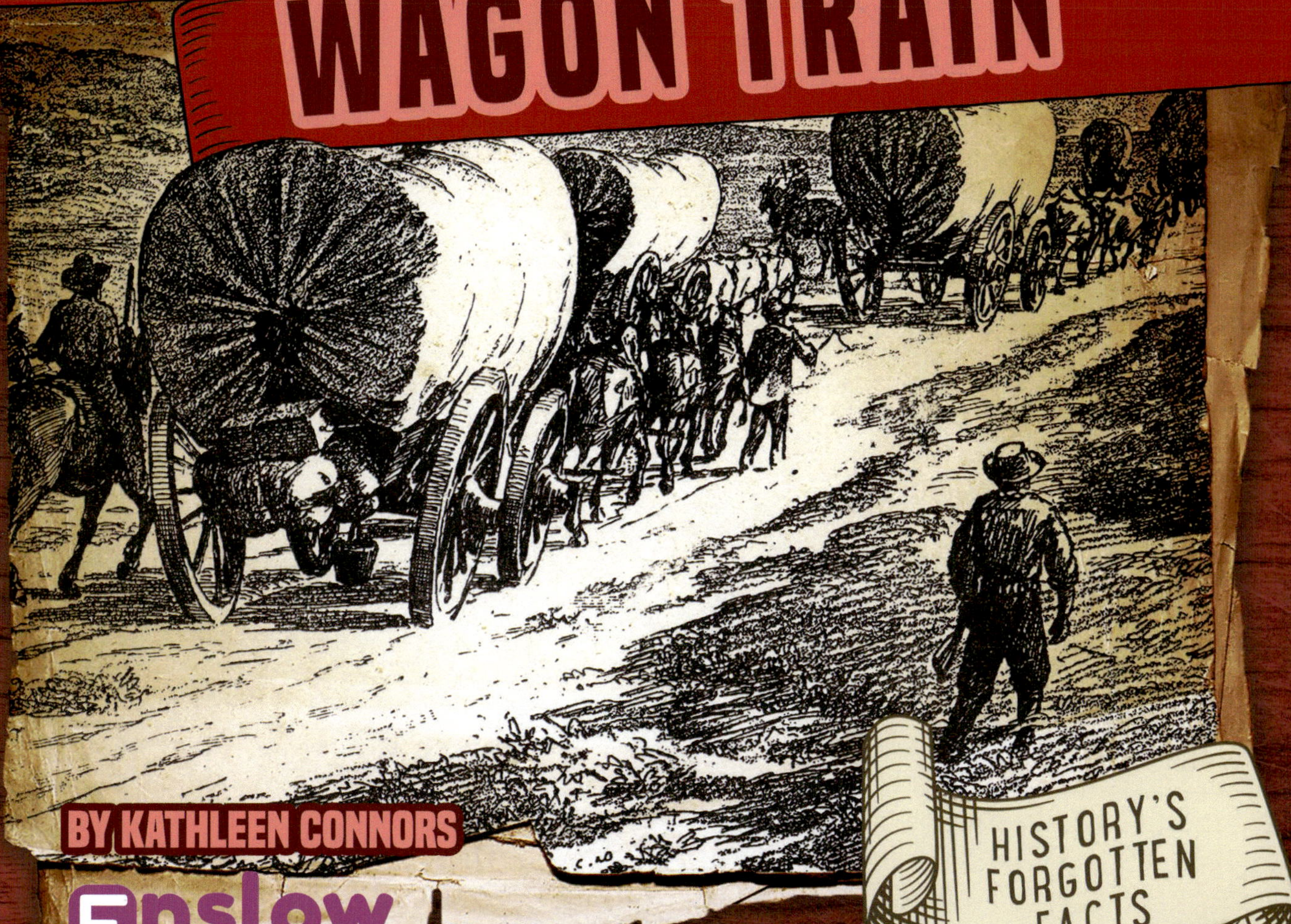

BY KATHLEEN CONNORS

Enslow PUBLISHING

HISTORY'S FORGOTTEN FACTS

Please visit our website, www.enslow.com. For a free color catalog of all our high-quality books, call toll free 1-800-398-2504 or fax 1-877-980-4454.

Library of Congress Cataloging-in-Publication Data
Names: Connors, Kathleen, author.
Title: Forgotten facts about life on a wagon train / Kathleen Connors.
Description: Buffalo, New York : Enslow Publishing, [2024] | Series: History's forgotten facts | Includes bibliographical references and index.
Identifiers: LCCN 2023029413 | ISBN 9781978537767 (library binding) | ISBN 9781978537750 (paperback) | ISBN 9781978537774 (ebook)
Subjects: LCSH: Overland journeys to the Pacific–Juvenile literature. | Wagon trains–West (U.S.)–Juvenile literature. | Frontier and pioneer life–West (U.S.)–Juvenile literature. | West (U.S.)–History–19th century–Juvenile literature.
Classification: LCC F593 .C725 2024 | DDC 978.02–dc23/eng/20230705
LC record available at https://lccn.loc.gov/2023029413

Published in 2024 by
Enslow Publishing
2544 Clinton Street
Buffalo, NY 14224

Portions of this work were originally authored by Kristen Rajczak and published as *Life on a Wagon Train*. All new material in this edition authored by Kathleen Connors.

Designer: Tanya Dellaccio Keeney
Editor: Kristen Nelson

Photo credits: Cover, series background (banners) Ledelena/Shutterstock.com; cover, series background (paper) Vitaly Korovin/Shutterstock.com; cover, series background (wood) Pataradon Luangtongkum/Shutterstock.com; cover bauhaus1000/iStock.com; p. 5 https://upload.wikimedia.org/wikipedia/commons/1/19/Oregontrail_1907.jpg; p. 6 https://commons.wikimedia.org/wiki/File:Pioneers_Crossing_the_Plains_of_Nebraska_by_C.C.A._Christensen.png; p. 7 Courtesy of The Library of Congress; p. 9 Christine_Kohler/iStock.com; p. 10 Gatien GREGORI/Shutterstock.com; p. 11 https://upload.wikimedia.org/wikipedia/commons/c/c0/Alfred_Jacob_Miller_-_Breaking_up_Camp_at_Sunrise_-_Walters_371940142.jpg; p. 13 https://upload.wikimedia.org/wikipedia/commons/6/6e/Bierstadt_Albert_Oregon_Trail.jpg; p. 15 https://upload.wikimedia.org/wikipedia/commons/7/70/ColumbiaAmericasGreatHighway040.png; p. 17 Everett Collection/Shutterstock.com; p. 19 Victorian Traditions/Shutterstock.com.

Printed in the United States of America

CPSIA compliance information: Batch #CWENS24: For further information contact Enslow Publishing at 1-800-398-2504.

CONTENTS

Words in the glossary appear in **bold** type the first time they are used in the text.

WESTWARD!

Traveling across the United States today can take a few days in a car. If you take a plane, it takes only about six hours to fly from New York City to Los Angeles. During the 1800s, however, it took about five months to travel from Missouri to Oregon!

THE OREGON TRAIL WAS ONE OF THE MOST POPULAR ROUTES FOR WAGON TRAINS TO TAKE, THOUGH IT WASN'T THE ONLY TRAIL. IT WAS ABOUT 2,170 MILES (3,492 KM) LONG.

Hundreds of thousands of Americans used covered wagons to cross the **frontier** from the 1840s to the 1880s. The journey was hard, but some saw it as an adventure!

DON'T FORGET!

The **routes** used by many wagon trains started as trails made by Native Americans.

GET ON THE TRAIN

People leaving their homes to live in another place, such as those in wagon trains, are called emigrants. Wagon trains were often made up of families and people from the same town. They might have had more than 100 wagons or as few as two or three.

SOME EMIGRANTS PAINTED THEIR WAGONS BRIGHT COLORS TO MAKE IT EASIER TO KEEP A GROUP TOGETHER ON THE TRAILS!

DON'T FORGET!

Traveling in a group was safer as there were more people to help with sickness, wagon repairs, and possible Native American attacks.

Men who had **explored** the frontier before, such as fur trappers, guided some wagon trains. Emigrants met these guides at several "jumping-off points," including places in Iowa and Missouri, before they began the journey west.

WHAT TO BRING

Emigrants left their whole lives—and a lot of their belongings—behind to travel west. Still, a packed wagon weighed about 2,500 pounds (1,134 kg)! Wagons were packed with food and supplies needed for the trip in addition to anything emigrants needed to settle in the West.

Families brought candles, tents, and tools to fix their wagon. They brought pans to cook in. Luckily, they didn't need to bring wood for cooking fires. Buffalo chips—or dried buffalo waste—burned quickly and easily!

DON'T FORGET!

While free and easy to find, buffalo chips weren't the best fuel for a fire. Two to three bushels were needed to heat one meal!

PEOPLE STARTING OUT WITH A WAGON TRAIN SOMETIMES CHOSE A LEADER AND MADE A LIST OF RULES EVERYONE HAD TO FOLLOW.

A LONG WALK

What animals could pull a heavy wagon the 12 to 20 miles (19 to 32 km) wagon trains traveled in a day? Emigrants bought mules, horses, or oxen to pull their wagon. Many chose oxen because they could pull heavier loads and cost less to care for. They were also less likely to be stolen by Native Americans.

DON'T FORGET!
An ox is a kind of male cow.

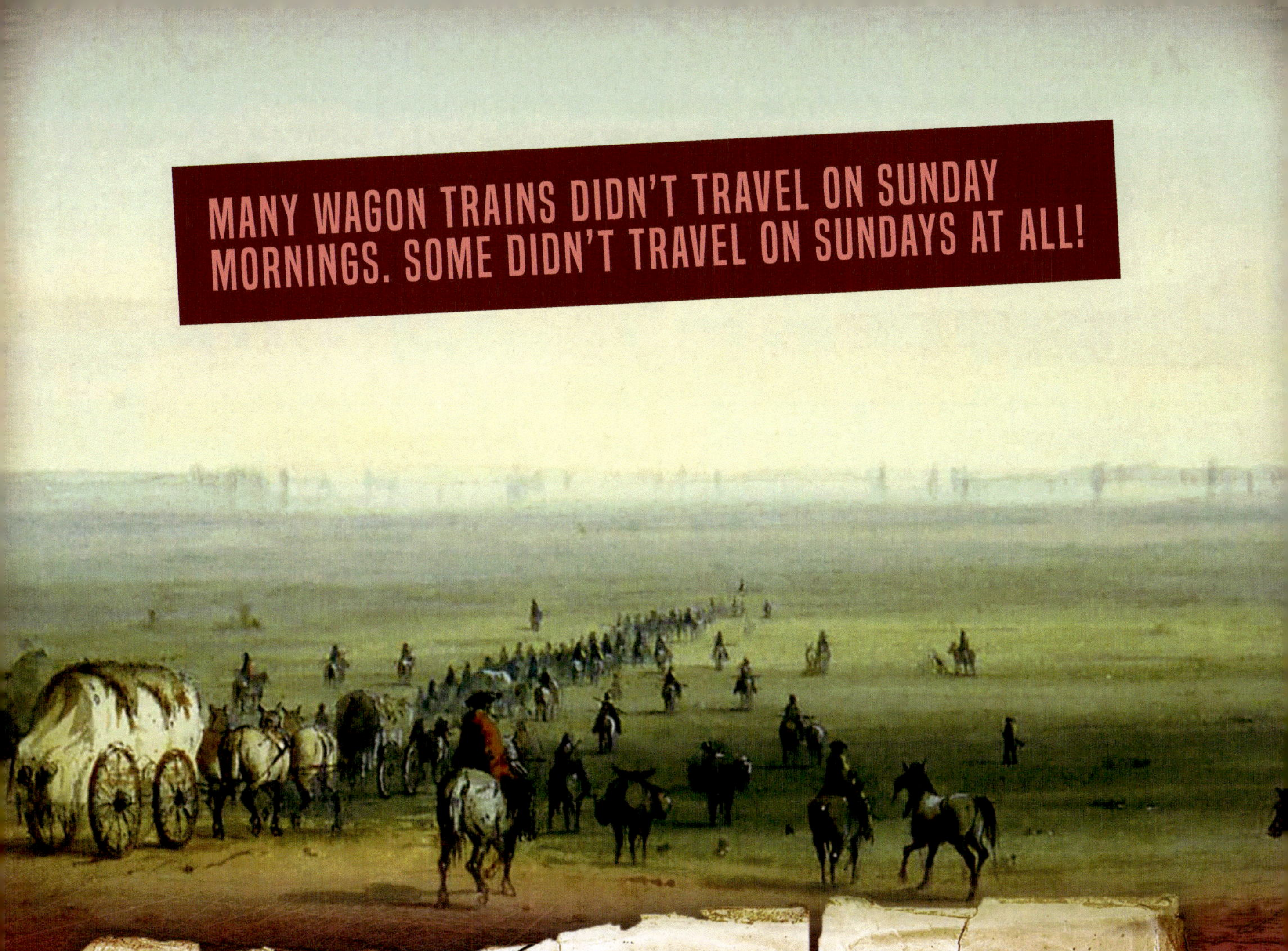

MANY WAGON TRAINS DIDN'T TRAVEL ON SUNDAY MORNINGS. SOME DIDN'T TRAVEL ON SUNDAYS AT ALL!

However, the oxen pulled wagons full of supplies—not people. Unless someone was very old or very sick, travelers walked next to the wagon.

BREAD AND BUTTER

Each family on the wagon train brought more than 1,000 pounds (454 kg) of food. Coffee, beans, and rice were common since they lasted a long time. The travelers soaked dried meat and fruit in water to make it soft enough to eat. Emigrants packed flour, sugar, and salt to make bread.

Many people brought cattle to have a source of milk. Families hooked buckets of cream under their wagon. The wagon bumped along the rough roads and **churned** it into butter!

DON'T FORGET!

Sheep and cattle traveling with the wagon train could become a source of food if needed. They also helped start herds on the frontier.

EMIGRANTS WENT TO BED AFTER DINNER ON THE TRAIL. THEY NEEDED A GOOD NIGHT'S REST FOR THE HARD JOURNEY THE NEXT DAY.

DANGER AND DEATH

On the way west, emigrants dealt with bad weather and had to cross dangerously fast rivers. Children and other slow travelers often got lost.

Drowning and other **accidents** were common too. Women's skirts got caught under wheels, pulling them under the wagon. People mistakenly fired guns at themselves and others. Families knew it was a risky journey, but most felt free farmland, possible gold, or just starting over in a new place was worth it.

ABOUT ONE IN 10 EMIGRANTS WHO TRAVELED THE OREGON TRAIL DIED ALONG THE WAY.

DON'T FORGET!

Men often brought guns along to hunt, and also to guard against Native American attacks. There were lots of gun accidents because many didn't know how to use the guns well.

SICKNESS SPREADS

People traveling by wagon train didn't have fresh fruits and vegetables. Without the **vitamin** C these provide, many suffered from an illness called scurvy. From 1849 to 1852, thousands of emigrants died from cholera, a sickness caused by **bacteria**. Historians think cholera spread because of the dirty conditions where people would stop for water.

Emigrants also faced smallpox, a sickness somewhat like chicken pox. Illnesses likes these were the most common cause of death on wagon trains.

DON'T FORGET!

Wagon trains often carried some medicines, or drugs used to treat sickness.

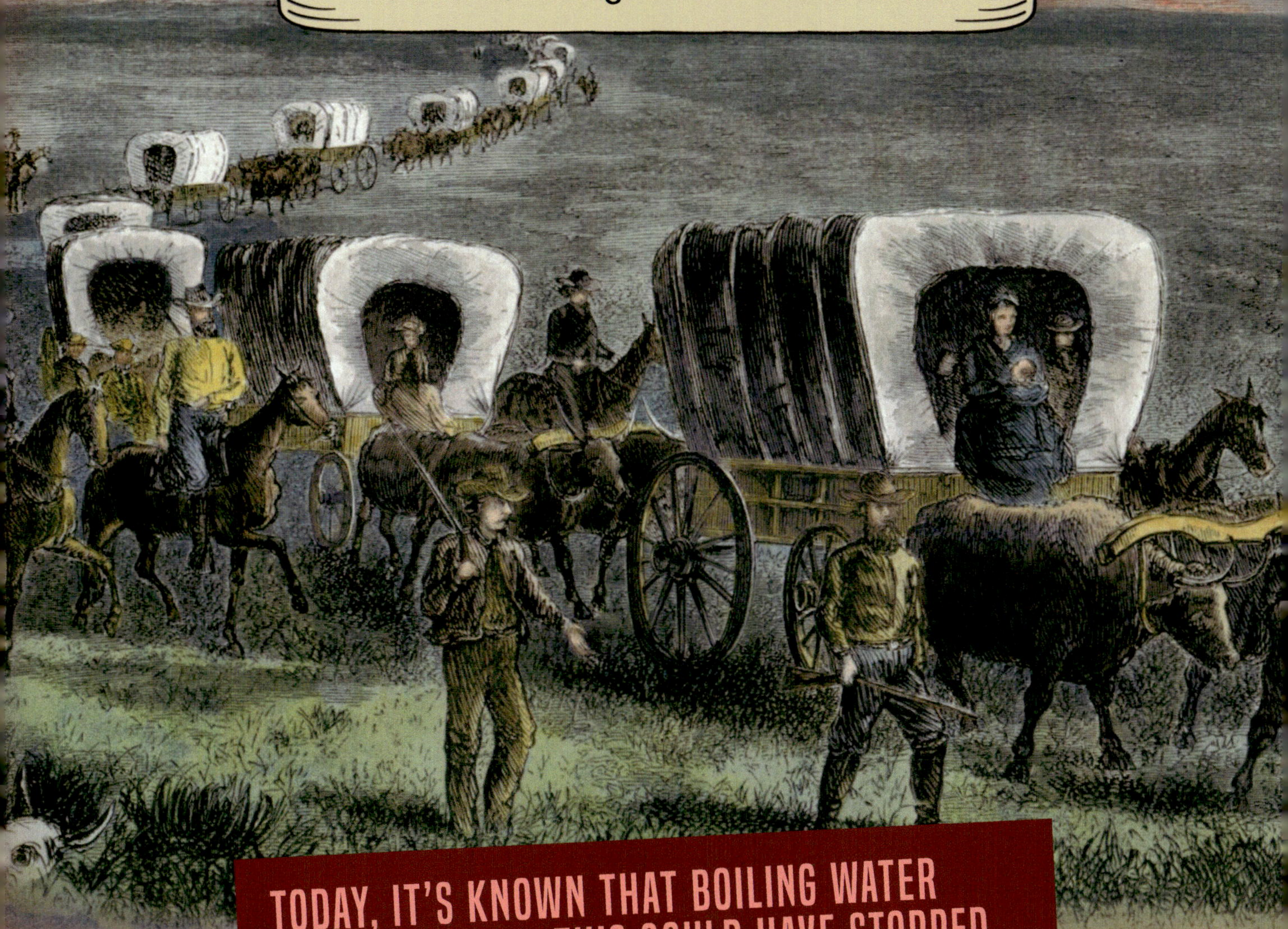

TODAY, IT'S KNOWN THAT BOILING WATER KILLS BACTERIA. THIS COULD HAVE STOPPED THE SPREAD OF CHOLERA AMONG EMIGRANTS.

LIFE GOES ON

Life on a wagon train wasn't always a struggle. Travelers found ways to have a good time. They sang and told stories around the campfire. They **celebrated** weddings at jumping off points and along the trail. Most wagon trains had many new babies born on the way west too!

Some children took months off from school while on the wagon train. Others still did schoolwork when the wagon train stopped for the day.

IN ORDER TO LIGHTEN A WAGON'S LOAD, FAMILIES WOUND UP LEAVING ALL SORTS OF THINGS ON THE SIDE OF THE ROAD, FROM FURNITURE TO FAMILY **HEIRLOOMS**.

DON'T FORGET!

Women often did **laundry** on Sundays. But, if emigrants found clean water, they might stop to do it then! This would take all day.

SENDING A MESSAGE

People on wagon trains left messages for emigrants coming after them. These messages might be for family or friends who left at a later date. They might be warnings to other travelers about dangerous paths or dirty water.

Wagon trains left messages on all sorts of things! They wrote on bark, rocks, and small pieces of cloth. We know so much about the emigrants on wagon trains because many travelers wrote diaries along the way too.

DON'T FORGET!

Letters could be mailed at military post offices along the route or given to groups traveling back east.

WHY DID EMIGRANTS GO WEST?

GOLD: IN 1848, MEN FOUND GOLD IN CALIFORNIA. THOUSANDS OF PEOPLE HEADED WEST HOPING TO STRIKE IT RICH.

FREEDOM: MEMBERS OF THE CHURCH OF JESUS CHRIST OF LATTER-DAY SAINTS WENT WEST TO ESCAPE **PERSECUTION**.

MANIFEST DESTINY: SOME AMERICANS THOUGHT IT WAS GOD'S WILL FOR THE UNITED STATES TO GROW.

NEW LIFE: EMIGRANTS OFTEN LEFT MONEY PROBLEMS BEHIND IN THE EAST.

CIVIL WAR: BY THE 1860S, THE NORTH AND SOUTH WERE FIGHTING. AMERICANS FLED THIS WAR BY GOING WEST.

FREE LAND: MANY TRAVELERS GOT FREE LAND IN OREGON. THEN, IN 1862, THE U.S. GOVERNMENT PASSED THE HOMESTEAD ACT. IT GAVE FARMERS FREE LAND IN PARTS OF THE WEST IF THEY FARMED IT FOR FIVE YEARS.

GLOSSARY

accident: An unexpected event that happens by chance.

bacteria: Tiny creatures that can be seen only with a microscope.

celebrate: To honor with special activities.

churn: To stir or shake forcefully.

explore: To search in order to find out new things.

frontier: A part of a country that has been newly opened for settlement.

heirloom: Something handed down through a family over many years.

laundry: Clothes to be washed.

persecution: Making a group of people suffer cruel or unfair treatment.

route: A course that people travel.

vitamin: A natural matter that is often found in foods and helps a body be healthy.

FOR MORE INFORMATION

Books

Goss, Elizabeth Ames. *My Way West: Real Kids Traveling the Oregon & California Trails*. Berkeley, CA: West Margin Press, 2021.

Rusick, Jessica. *Enduring the Oregon Trail: A This or That Debate*. North Mankato, MN: Capstone Press, 2021.

Websites

Kids Listen: Oregon Trail
https://app.kidslisten.org/ep/Bedtime-History-Inspirational-Stories-for-Kids-and-Families-Oregon-Trail
Check out this podcast for kids about the Oregon Trail.

The Oregon Trail Game Online
www.visitoregon.com/the-oregon-trail-game-online/
Play an online version of a computer game about the Oregon Trail. Read more about how it came to be and who traveled it.

INDEX